I don't want to go to bed!

by Julie Sykes

illustrated by Tim Warnes

Translated by East Word

小老虎很淘氣。
他不愛上床睡覺。
每當晚上虎媽媽說："該睡覺了！"
小老虎就會嚷著："可是我不想睡覺！"

Little Tiger was very naughty.
He did not like going to bed.
Every night when Mummy Tiger said,
'Bedtime!'
Little Tiger would say,
'But I don't *want* to go to bed!'

小老虎不讓媽媽幫他洗澡，也不肯聽媽媽講故事。一天晚上，虎媽媽發脾氣了。

當小老虎又說他不想睡覺時，虎媽媽生氣地說：

"好吧！你從此不用睡覺了！"

Little Tiger wouldn't let Mummy Tiger clean him, and he wouldn't listen to his bedtime story. One night Mummy Tiger lost her temper. When Little Tiger said, 'I don't want to go to bed!' she roared, 'ALL RIGHT, YOU CAN STAY UP ALL NIGHT!'

小老虎高興得簡直不敢相信自己的耳朵，
他蹦蹦跳跳地跑進森林，生怕虎媽媽
改變主意把他叫回去。

Little Tiger couldn't believe his good luck.
He scampered off into the jungle
before Mummy Tiger could
change her mind.

小老虎去找他最要好的朋友：小獅子。
當他來到小獅子家裡的時候，小獅子正
在洗他的耳朵呢。
"現在是該睡覺的時候了，" 獅爸爸威
嚴地呵道。 "你怎麼還不睡覺?"

Little Tiger went to visit his best
friend, Little Lion. When he arrived,
Little Lion was having his ears washed.
'It's bedtime,' growled Daddy Lion.
'Why are you still up?'

"我不想睡覺！" 小老虎答道，趁著獅子爸爸也
幫他洗耳朵之前，小老虎一下子跳進了森林。

'I don't want to go to bed!' said Little Tiger,
and he skipped off into the jungle before
Daddy Lion could wash his ears, too!

小老虎決定去找他的第二個好朋友：小河馬。
他看見小河馬正在河裡高興地洗睡前澡呢！

Little Tiger decided to visit his second best friend,
Little Hippo. He found him splashing in the river,
having a bedtime bath.

"是該睡覺的時候了，" 河馬爸爸説， "你怎麼還没睡？"
"我不想睡覺！" 小老虎説著像一陣風似地跑回了森林裡，
不然河馬爸爸也會給他洗澡了。

'It's bedtime,' bellowed Daddy Hippo. 'Why are you still up?'
'I don't want to go to bed!' said Little Tiger, and he scurried off into
the jungle before Daddy Hippo could give him a bath, too!

小象是小老虎的第三個好朋友，於是小老虎又去找小象。小象沒有在外面玩，他躺在床上，聽他的睡前故事呢。"該睡覺了，"象媽媽對小老虎說，"你怎麼還沒睡？"
"我不想睡覺！"小老虎說著跳回了森林，就怕象媽媽也要他睡覺。

Little Elephant was Little Tiger's third best friend. He went to visit him next. Little Elephant was not out playing. He was in bed, listening to his bedtime story. 'It's bedtime,' trumpeted Mummy Elephant. 'Why are you still up?'
'I don't want to go to bed!' said Little Tiger, and he bounced off into the jungle before Mummy Elephant could put him to bed, too!

小老虎又想：我可以去找小猴 — 他的第四個好朋友。但是他卻只看見猴媽媽。猴媽媽把食指放在嘴唇上，悄聲說："噓，小猴已經睡著了。你怎麼還不去睡？"

Little Tiger thought he would go and find Little Monkey, his fourth best friend. But he found Mummy Monkey first. She put a finger to her lips and whispered, 'Little Monkey is fast asleep. Why are you still up?'

"我不想睡覺！" 小老虎低聲答道。
然後在猴媽媽把他也弄睡著之前，
便悄悄地溜回森林中去了。

'I don't want to go to bed!' Little
Tiger whispered back. Quickly
he tiptoed into the jungle before
Mummy Monkey made him fall
asleep, too!

小老虎沒有什麼地方可以去了。他從來沒有單獨在森林裡呆到這麼晚過。
就連太陽都睡覺去了。天突然變得特別黑。*那是什麼？*

Little Tiger didn't know where to go next. He had never been
alone on his own in the jungle so late before. Even the sun
had gone to bed! Suddenly it seemed very dark. *What was that?*

小老虎抬頭一看……

Little Tiger looked up
and saw . . .

……一雙大大的黃色眼睛
在盯著他！

. . . two very large yellow eyes
staring back at him!

那是夜猴的眼睛。
"你為什麼沒有睡覺？" 她問小老虎。
"我不想睡覺，" 小老虎勇敢地回答，
"你不是也沒睡嘛！"
"那是因為我在太陽升起來以後才
睡覺呢。" 夜猴告訴小老虎。

The eyes belonged to a bush baby.
'Shouldn't you be in bed?' she asked.
'I don't want to go to bed,' said Little
Tiger bravely. '*You* haven't!'
'That's because I go to bed when the
sun rises,' said Bush Baby.

"在暖洋洋的陽光下怎可以睡一覺！"
小老虎不禁打了個寒戰，他沒想到
夜晚的森林會是這麼黑、這麼冷。

'Fancy going to bed in the lovely
sunshine!' thought Little Tiger.
He shivered and thought how
cold and dark it was in the jungle
at night.

"我帶你回家吧！" 夜猴說，"你媽媽會擔心的。"
"我不想回家，我不想睡覺！" 小老虎喊著。但是他也不想一個人留在黑乎乎的森林裡。

'I'm taking you home,' said Bush Baby. 'Your mummy will be worried.'
'I don't want to go home! I don't want to go to bed!' said Little Tiger.
But he didn't want to be left in the dark either.

小老虎只好跟著夜猴回家。他很高興有夜猴明亮的大眼睛幫他照亮回家的路。
"我們就快到了，" 夜猴說著。小老虎無可奈何地慢吞吞地跟在後面。

So Little Tiger followed Bush Baby home. He was glad of her big
bright eyes to show him the way.
'Nearly there,' said Bush Baby, as LittleTiger dragged slowly behind.

"我不想…" 小老虎一邊睡意矇矓地嘟噥著，一邊拖著他困倦的腳步。
"噢，你回來啦，" 虎媽媽看見小老虎對他說，"正好趕得及睡覺。"

'I don't want to go to . . .' said Little Tiger sleepily, dragging
his paws.
'Ah, there you are,' said Mummy Tiger. 'Just in time for bed!'

"我不想⋯" 小老虎打著哈欠，説了半句就睡著了！
老虎媽媽安頓好小老虎後，轉身去找夜猴。

'I don't want to . . .' yawned Little Tiger, and he fell fast asleep!
Mummy Tiger tucked him up and then turned to Bush Baby . . .

但房子裡已空無一人，夜猴已經躲到
森林裡不見了，好像怕虎媽媽也要她睡覺。

. . . but the den was empty. Bush Baby
had disappeared into the jungle before
Mummy Tiger could tuck *her* up, too!